DETECTIVE VALENTINE

To Abigail, Adam, and Shae

Detective Valentine
Copyright © 1987 by Audrey Wood
Printed in the U.S.A. All rights reserved.

Library of Congress Cataloging-in-Publication Data
Wood, Audrey.
   Detective Valentine.

   Summary: The great Detective Valentine has his work
cut out for him when the Snow Queen's crown is stolen
two days before the contest and the mayor's wife,
a famous actress, and the detective's good friend are
all suspects.

   [1. Mystery and detective stories]   I. Title.
PZ7.W846De 1987   [E]   86-45784
ISBN 0-06-026599-X
ISBN 0-06-026600-7 (lib. bdg.)

1 2 3 4 5 6 7 8 9 10
First Edition

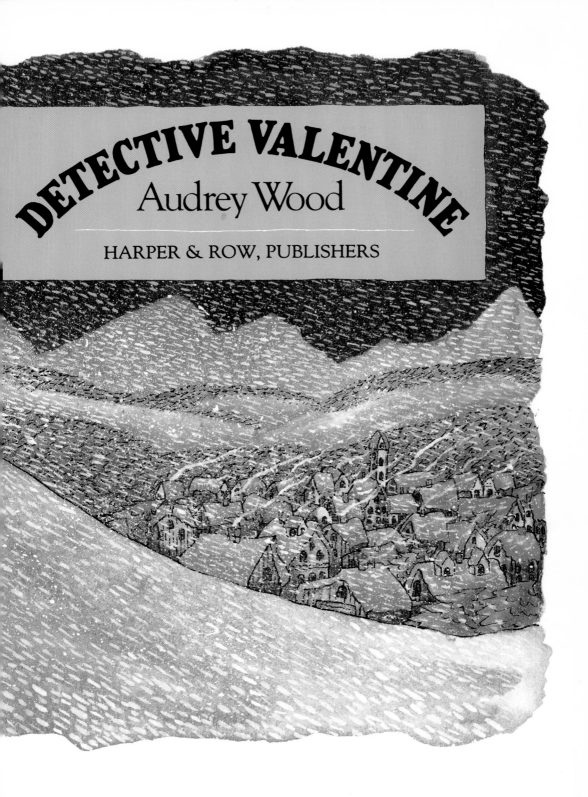

DETECTIVE VALENTINE

Audrey Wood

HARPER & ROW, PUBLISHERS

It was almost midnight when the mystery began. With a chilling blast, Old North Wind blew snow over the rooftops of Bigalowville. High on a hill, one light still burned brightly. In the cozy bungalow of the great Detective Valentine, a search was underway.

"Piffle!" Valentine muttered. "I can't go out tomorrow without a hat. A detective must keep his brain warm."

Valentine peered beneath his rug and, at last, found his missing ski hat. He moved his chair away from the wall, pulled his toolbox out from behind the chair, and hammered a nail into the wall.

"There," he said, hanging his ski hat on the nail. "Now you won't get lost again!"

Just then the grandfather clock began to strike
midnight.

Suddenly the door blew open.

Valentine heard an eerie scream.

"Eeeooooo!"

Grabbing his lantern, the brave detective rushed
outside, but all he found was snow.

Hmmm, he thought. That eerie scream must have
been Old North Wind howling through the trees.

He hurried back inside, locked his door, and went
to sleep.

"Help! Help!" called a frantic voice early the next morning. Mayor Bigalow entered the house with a gust of wind. "Tomorrow is the Snow Queen contest," he cried, "and someone has stolen the queen's crown! You must solve this mystery, Detective!"

"I'll take the case," Valentine said. Then he reached for his hat on the nail.

"Hufty McGufty!" he exclaimed. "My ski hat is missing!

"Facts," the great detective said, counting on his fingers. "One. Hat hung on nail. Two. Clock struck midnight. Three. Eerie scream.

"By gumbo!" he exclaimed. "That scream last night was a trick. When I went outside, a thief sneaked in and stole my hat."

"Come now," the mayor said. "If you must have a ski hat, we'll stop by my place. Mrs. Bigalow collects hats. I'm sure she'll lend you one."

"A hat collector," Valentine said, racing out the door. "A likely suspect!"

"Wait!" the mayor called. "What about the stolen crown?"

Valentine pushed off on his sled. "Not now!" he called back. "I'm on The Case of the Missing Hat."

As Detective Valentine sped down the hill, an icy wind whistled about his ears. "Brrr." He shivered. "My head feels like an ice cube."

He took off a glove, put it on his head, and pulled it down over his ears.

"Ahhh," he sighed.

The glove felt warm and toasty.

Soon the clever detective arrived at the mayor's mansion and found Mrs. Bigalow in the library.

"Mind answering a few questions?" he asked, taking out his notebook and pencil. "Isn't it true that you collect hats?"

"Why, yes indeed," Mrs. Bigalow said. "I simply can't find enough to keep me happy."

"And," Valentine continued, "isn't it true that you are the wicked thief?"

Mrs. Bigalow burst into tears. "It's true! It's true!" she sobbed.

Valentine offered his handkerchief. "Just tell me the facts," he said.

"It's all Lily Pomp's fault." Mrs. Bigalow sniffed. "She's that actress at the Winter Theater. Lily Pomp told the mayor it wasn't fair for me to be Snow Queen five years in a row. I was afraid he wouldn't choose me again, so I stole the Snow Queen crown."

"Crown?" Valentine exclaimed.

Mrs. Bigalow hurried to the fireplace. "The crown,"
she said, "is hidden in this secret wall safe." She
touched a painting above the mantel.

The painting swung out from the wall.

"It's gone!" she gasped. "Someone has stolen my
crown!"

Detective Valentine hurried out the door.

"Stop!" Mrs. Bigalow cried. "What about my stolen
crown?"

"Not now," Valentine called back. "I'm on The
Case of the Missing Hat."

That evening, as darkness fell, Detective Valentine entered Rosie's Cafe.

Rosie had never seen the detective looking more discouraged. With a cheery smile, she handed him a Dinner Special and a cup of hot chocolate.

"Looks like you're working on a tough case," she said. "Anything I can do to help?"

"Thanks," Valentine said. "Know anything strange about hats?"

Rosie glanced at the glove on his head, but decided not to mention it.

"I'm entering the Snow Queen contest," she said. "Do you think that's strange?"

"Interesting," the detective said. "Very interesting."

After dinner Valentine returned to his bungalow. "No clues on The Case of the Missing Hat," he sighed. The detective hung his glove on the nail.

He took off his boots and fell asleep with his clothes still on.

17

The next day Valentine awoke with a cold head. Old
North Wind was blowing through an open window,
and the glove on the nail was gone.

"Hufty McGufty!" he shouted. "The wicked thief sneaked in again!"

Valentine sat up and pulled on one of his boots. "I must have a hat," he said. "My head feels like an icicle."

The detective picked up his other boot, turned it upside down, and pulled it over his ears.

"Ahhh," he sighed.

The boot felt warm and toasty.

But what about my foot? he thought.

Valentine found an old tennis shoe, put it on, and tromped out into the snow. He picked up the morning newspaper and read the headlines.

SNOW QUEEN
CROWN STOLEN

• • •

CONCERNED MAYOR FORCED

TO CANCEL SNOW QUEEN CONTEST

Just then Lily Pomp sledded past Valentine's bungalow. Her sled hit a bump, bouncing a large handbag out into the snow.

Valentine reached down and picked up the bag.

"That's mine!" Lily Pomp shouted, dragging her sled back up the hill. "Give it to me!"

"So you're the actress at the Winter Theater," Valentine said, handing her the bag.

"Would you like an autograph?" She smiled, fluttering her long lashes.

"I'm looking for a wicked thief," Valentine said.

"I wouldn't call her wicked," Lily Pomp said, jumping into her sled. "She's beautiful, and her crime was daring."

"*Her* crime!" the detective exclaimed. "So you're the criminal!"

Lily Pomp took off on her sled. "You'll never catch me," she called.

"Halt!" Valentine shouted. "Crime never pays!"

The detective quickly jumped aboard his sled and pushed off. The chase was on.

Down the hill they sped, faster and faster.

"Help!" Lily Pomp shouted. "I can't stop my sled!"
"I can't stop mine either!" Valentine shouted back.
Together they raced out of control toward Rosie's
Cafe.

"Look out!" Lily Pomp screamed as they crashed through Rosie's door.

Mrs. Bigalow and Rosie dove beneath a table. Lily Pomp's bag flew across the room and knocked Mayor Bigalow over the counter. Old North Wind followed with a blast of icy air.

Detective Valentine stood up. "All right, Pomp!"
he announced. "Hand over the stolen goods!"

Lily Pomp found her bag and held it up. "It's in
here," she said. "I'm glad I stole it. I'd do it again if I
had the chance."

Then the actress looked inside her bag.

"It's gone!" she cried, fainting into Valentine's arms.

"Thunderation!" the detective exclaimed.

Lily Pomp opened one eye. "Yesterday morning I went to see the mayor," she explained. "I wanted him to make me the next Snow Queen. As I waited in the library, I touched a painting over the fireplace, and..."

"Of course," Valentine interrupted. "You stole the Snow Queen crown."

"Yes," Lily Pomp said, "and now it's been stolen from me."

"I want my crown!" Mrs. Bigalow cried.

"Where can it be?" the mayor demanded.

"What a mess!" Rosie said.

"Silence!" Valentine boomed. "I will now solve The Mystery of the Stolen Crown once and for all!

"Facts," Valentine said, counting on his fingers.

"One. Mrs. Bigalow stole the crown from Mayor Bigalow."

"Oh, my dear!" the mayor exclaimed. "How could you!"

"Two," Valentine said. "Lily Pomp stole the crown from Mrs. Bigalow."

"It's a crime wave!" the mayor gasped.

"Now," Valentine continued, "the crown has been stolen from Lily Pomp—and," he added, "the thief is in this room."

Mrs. Bigalow looked at Rosie.

Rosie looked at Lily Pomp.

Lily Pomp looked at Detective Valentine.

Detective Valentine reached over and slowly removed the mayor's top hat. There, perched on the Mayor's head, was the Snow Queen crown.

Everyone stared in wonder.

"I don't understand," Pomp said. "Why did the
mayor steal the crown?"

"If he crowns Mrs. Bigalow Snow Queen, everyone
is angry," Valentine explained.

"If he crowns someone else, Mrs. Bigalow is angry,"
Rosie said.

"No crown, no contest, no one is angry," the mayor
cried. "I liked the idea of not having a Snow Queen.

"Oh, woe is me," the mayor moaned. "Now I must
judge the contest."

"Hurray for Detective Valentine!" Mrs. Bigalow
cheered. "I'll win again!"

But the detective had a plan. He put the crown on his sled and pulled it up the hill to his home.

"Piffle!" he said as he entered his bungalow.

Valentine threw the boot on his head across the room.

"The great detective solves The Mystery of the Stolen Crown three times," he said, "but can't solve The Case of the Missing Hat once!"

Valentine hung the Snow Queen crown on the nail.

"Ooooeeeeee!"
Old North Wind howled through the trees.
Bang! The door blew open.

Tunk.

The crown blew off the nail and fell down
behind the detective's chair.

Valentine leaned over and gazed down at the crown, the missing ski hat, and the missing glove.

"Flusternation!" he said. "Old North Wind was the wicked thief. The Case of the Missing Hat is solved."

That evening, as Old North Wind blew snow over the rooftops of Bigalowville, Detective Valentine judged the Snow Queen contest and crowned the new Snow Queen.

And after the contest, Rosie treated everyone to
snowball ice cream and hot chocolate.